Contents

Feeling shy

Most people feel shy sometimes.
You might get the feeling if...

...you go
somewhere
without your
family.

...you go to a
big occasion
where there are
lots of grown-ups.

SHY

...you go to your
friend's birthday
party but it's very
noisy and busy.

...you go to
your friend's
house and meet
new people there.

...you go to a
playground where
there are children
you don't know.

Everybody Feels...
SHY

Moira Harvey
& Holly Sterling

Quarto is the authority on a wide range of topics.

Quarto educates, entertains and enriches the lives of our readers—enthusiasts and lovers of hands-on living.

www.quartoknows.com

Author: Moira Harvey
Illustrator: Holly Sterling
Designer: Mike Henson
Editor: Carly Madden
Consultant: Cecilia Essau

A catalogue record for this book is available from the British Library.

ISBN 978-0-7112-5042-0

Manufactured in Guangzhou, China EB052020

9 8 7 6 5 4 3 2 1

How it feels

You want to curl up
like a snail in a shell
shrinking small
so no one can see you.

Your words are whispers.
You're a little bit scared.
You are feeling...

shy.

Poppy feels shy

One day I went to a wedding party where there were lots of grown-ups. I took my doll, Amy.

Look at all those people, Amy!

6

I felt so shy I hid behind
my Mum and Dad.

I wish
I could go
home.

7

Later, a lady asked me my name.
I whispered it because **I** felt so shy.

"My name
is Poppy."

Then it was time
for some food.
"Let's show Amy the
wedding cake," said Mum.

Isn't that
pretty, Amy!

9

There was some music, too.
"Let's show Amy how to dance," said Dad.

I think Amy liked dancing.

It was easier to do things with
Amy, instead of on my own.
It helped me feel less shy.

I had a good
time at the
wedding!

Mateo feels shy

One day I went to Poppy's birthday party. It was noisy and everybody was running around. I felt a little bit scared.

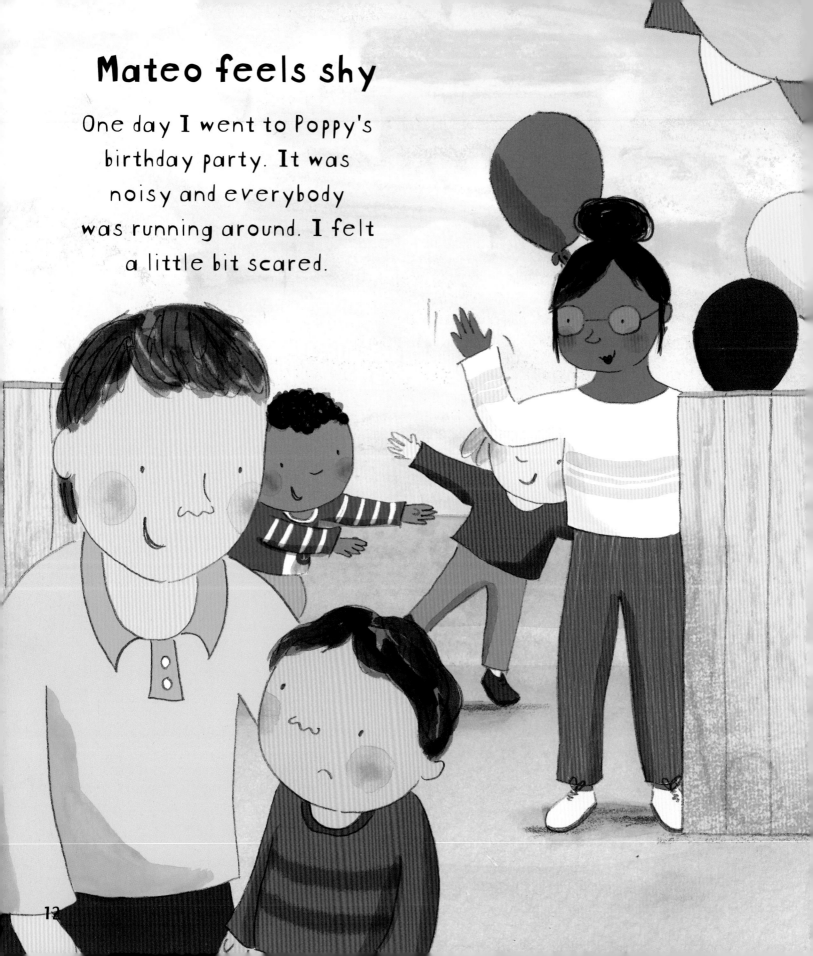

The other children played
a game, but I didn't.

I didn't want to let go
of my Dad's hand.

"Don't worry. I'll help you play the next game," said Dad.

It was a game of *Pass the Parcel*.

My Dad made everybody
laugh. I laughed, too.

"Oops!
Silly me!"

Then it was my turn to hit a piñata.
I did it all on my own!

"Great job, Mateo!"

I felt happier, so I joined in some more games on my own.

I had a good time at the party!

Feeling better

Poppy went to a wedding where there were lots of grown-ups. She felt very shy but she took her doll Amy with her and that made things easier.

Mateo went to his friend's birthday party but he felt shy. His Dad helped him to join in a game and that made it easier than joining in on his own.

Poppy and Mateo both found that their shy feeling went away when they began to enjoy themselves.

Poppy's story

1 Poppy went to a wedding where there were lots of grown-ups. She felt very shy.

2 She took her doll Amy with her.

3 Amy kept her company and helped her do things.

4 Poppy began to enjoy herself and her shy feeling went away.

Mateo's story

1 Mateo went to his friend's birthday party.

2 At first he felt too shy to join in the games.

3 His Dad helped him play a game, and it was fun.

4 Mateo started joining in and enjoying the party.

Story words

curl up

To hunch up your arms and legs. You might feel like doing this when you are shy, to make yourself seem smaller.

easier

When something isn't as difficult as it was before. Things got easier for Poppy and Mateo.

join in

To do something with other people. It can be hard to join in if you are feeling shy.

meet

When you meet someone you talk to them for the first time.

happier

When you feel better. Poppy and Mateo both felt happier when they relaxed and enjoyed themselves.

helped

When you are being helped, someone or something makes things easier for you.

scared
When something makes you jump or you feel unsafe.

shrinking
Getting smaller. You might feel like doing this when you are shy.

whispers
Words spoken very quietly. You might whisper when you feel shy.

occasion
An important event where there are lots of people. Poppy went to a wedding and Mateo went to a children's birthday party.

quietly
Speaking very softly, so it's hard to hear. You might do this when you feel shy.

Next steps

The stories in this book have been written to give children an introduction to feeling shy through events that they are familiar with. Here are some ideas to help you explore the feelings from the story together.

Talking

- Discuss how Poppy felt. She went to a big occasion where there was a roomful of grown-ups.
- Discuss how Mateo felt. He went to a birthday party where it was noisy and other children were running around.
- Talk about how Poppy and Mateo overcame their shy feeling. They both felt better when they began to relax and enjoy themselves.
- Look at page 4. Everybody is shy sometimes. Can your child think of times this has happened to them?
- Talk about how feeling shy makes people behave. Poppy whispered when she spoke. Mateo didn't want to let go of his Dad's hand.
- Look at the poem on page 5. You could help your child to write their own poem about what it's like to feel shy.

Make up a story

On pages 20-21 the stories have been broken down into four-stage sequences. Use this as a model to work together, making a simple sequence of events about somebody feeling shy and then feeling better. Ask your child to suggest the sequence of events and a way to resolve their story at the end.

An art session

Do a drawing session related to the feelings in this book. Here are some suggestions for drawings:

- A shy animal such as a snail curled up in his shell.
- The unhappy face of someone who feels shy, among a crowd of happy faces.
- A child enjoying themselves at a birthday party.

An acting session

Choose a scene and act it out, for example:

- Poppy and her doll Amy arriving at the wedding, then joining in the dancing.
- Mateo arriving at the party and then joining in a game, such as hitting a piñata.